he park, Spot.
today.

Come on, Spot

What are you doing?

Wait for us

Spot.

Helen! Spot the

Don't chase pigeons!

Oops!
Where did the
ball go?

Spot likes to swing.

Who is
Spot waving to?

Spot and Helen
with Tom.

play ball

Splash!

Look! The ball
is coming back,
Spot!